Dear Parents:

Congratulations! Your child is taking the first steps on an exciting journey. The destination? Independent reading!

STEP INTO READING® will help your child get there. The program offers five steps to reading success. Each step includes fun stories and colorful art or photographs. In addition to original fiction and books with favorite characters, there are Step into Reading Non-Fiction Readers, Phonics Readers and Boxed Sets, Sticker Readers, and Comic Readers—a complete literacy program with something to interest every child.

Learning to Read, Step by Step!

Ready to Read   Preschool–Kindergarten
• big type and easy words • rhyme and rhythm • picture clues
For children who know the alphabet and are eager to begin reading.

Reading with Help   Preschool–Grade 1
• basic vocabulary • short sentences • simple stories
For children who recognize familiar words and sound out new words with help.

Reading on Your Own   Grades 1–3
• engaging characters • easy-to-follow plots • popular topics
For children who are ready to read on their own.

Reading Paragraphs   Grades 2–3
• challenging vocabulary • short paragraphs • exciting stories
For newly independent readers who read simple sentences with confidence.

Ready for Chapters   Grades 2–4
• chapters • longer paragraphs • full-color art
For children who want to take the plunge into chapter books but still like colorful pictures.

STEP INTO READING® is designed to give every child a successful reading experience. The grade levels are only guides; children will progress through the steps at their own speed, developing confidence in their reading.

Remember, a lifetime love of reading starts with a single step!

Step into Reading, Random House, and the Random House colophon are registered trademarks of Penguin Random House LLC.

Visit us on the Web!
StepIntoReading.com
rhcbooks.com

Educators and librarians, for a variety of teaching tools, visit us at RHTeachersLibrarians.com

ISBN 978-0-7364-4011-0 (trade) — ISBN 978-0-7364-8281-3 (lib. bdg.)
ISBN 978-0-7364-4012-7 (ebook)

Printed in the United States of America   10 9 8 7 6 5 4 3 2 1

Disney · PIXAR

TOY STORY 4

OLD FRIENDS, NEW FRIENDS

by Natasha Bouchard

illustrated by the Disney Storybook Art Team

Random House 🏠 New York

Old friend.

New friend.

What makes
a good friend?

A friend is nice.

Woody welcomes Forky.

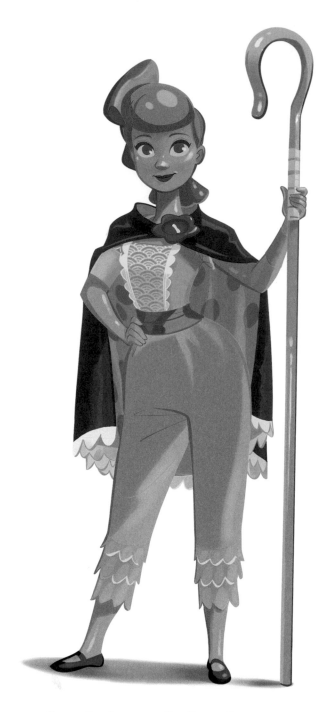

A friend is brave.

Bo Peep saves

the day.

A friend is loyal.

Buzz comes

to the rescue!

Ducky and Bunny
are funny friends!

Bo helps Woody.

Duke Caboom jumps
to help his friends.

A friend is caring.
Bo takes care
of her sheep.

Woody takes care
of Forky.

A friend is kind.

Gabby Gabby likes hugs.

A friend is special.

Forky makes

Bonnie happy.

Old friends.

New friends.

Friends are the best.